LITTLE MISS NAUGHTY

by Roger Hargreaves

EGMONT

Are you ever naughty?

Sometimes, I bet!

Well, Little Miss Naughty was naughty all the time.

She awoke one Sunday morning and looked out of the window.

"Looks like a nice day," she thought to herself.

And then she grinned.

"Looks like a nice day for being naughty," she said.

And rubbed her hands!

First thing on Monday morning the Mr Men had
a meeting.

"Something has to be done," announced Mr Uppity,
who had managed to straighten out his hat.

They all looked at Mr Clever, who was wearing his
spare pair of glasses.

"You're the cleverest," they said. "What's to be done
about Little Miss Naughty?"

Mr Clever thought. He cleared his throat. And spoke.

"I've no idea," he said.

"I have," piped up Mr Small.

"I know what that naughty little lady needs,"
he went on.

"And I know who can do it," he added.

"What?" asked Mr Uppity.

"Who?" asked Mr Clever.

"Aha!" chuckled Mr Small, and went off to see
a friend of his.

Somebody who could do impossible things.

Somebody who could do impossible things like
making himself invisible.

I wonder who that could be?

That Monday Mr Nosey was asleep under a tree.

Little Miss Naughty crept towards him with a pot of paint in one hand, a paintbrush in the other, and a rather large grin on her face.

She was going to paint the end of his nose!

Red!

But.

Just as she was about to do the dreadful deed, something happened.

TWEAK!

Somebody tweaked her nose!

Somebody she couldn't see tweaked her nose!

Somebody invisible!

I wonder who?

"Ouch!" cried Little Miss Naughty.

And, dropping the paint and paintbrush, she ran away as fast as her little legs would carry her.

On Tuesday Mr Busy was rushing along.

As usual!

Little Miss Naughty, standing by the side of the road, stuck out her foot.

She was going to trip him up!

Head over heels!

And heels over head!

But.

Just before she did, something happened.

TWEAK!

The invisible nose tweaker had struck again!

And it hurt!

"Ouch!" cried Little Miss Naughty.

And ran away even faster than her little legs would carry her.

On Wednesday Mr Happy was at home.

Watching television.

Outside, Little Miss Naughty picked up a stone.

She was going to break his window!

Naughty girl!

But.

As she brought her arm back to throw, guess what?

That's right!

TWEAK!

"Ouch!" cried Little Miss Naughty as she ran off, holding her nose.

And so it went on.

All day Thursday. TWEAK!

All day Friday. TWEAK! TWEAK!

All day Saturday. TWEAK! TWEAK! TWEAK!

By which time Little Miss Naughty's nose was bright red.

But.

By Sunday she was cured.

No naughtiness at all!

Thanks to the invisible nose tweaker.

On Sunday evening Mr Small went round to see him.

"Hello, Mr Impossible," he smiled.

"Thank you for helping to cure Little Miss Naughty."

"My pleasure," laughed Mr Impossible.

"But it did take all week."

Mr Small grinned.

"Don't you mean," he said, "all tweak?"